TEDDY BEAR STORYTIME

Contents

Material in this edition was previously published
in *Teddy Bear Tales*.

A catalogue record for this book is available from the British Library

Published by Ladybird Books Ltd
A subsidiary of the Penguin Group
A Pearson Company
© LADYBIRD BOOKS LTD MCMXCVII

LADYBIRD and the device of a Ladybird are trademarks of
Ladybird Books Ltd Loughborough Leicestershire UK

Ladybird

TEDDY BEAR STORYTIME

Chosen by Ronne Randall
Illustrated by Peter Stevenson

The Bear at the Bus Stop

"Look, Dad," cried the girl. "Someone's left their teddy at the bus stop."

"So they have," said Dad. "Do you think we should take him home with us?"

"Oh no!" cried the girl. "What if his owner comes back and Teddy isn't here?"

Just then the bus came. And the girl and her dad disappeared.

Before the next bus came, a lady came along. She was on her way to a jumble sale.

"Wouldn't you look nice on my Book and Toy Stall!" she told Teddy. But then she thought again.

"I'm sure your owner will be here very soon," she said. "So here's one of my books to sit on, to make you more comfortable while you wait."

6

Before the next bus, a childminder arrived. The children she was looking after squealed and pointed. "I want that bear!" they cried together.

But the childminder was firm. "That bear belongs to someone else," she said. "But I'm sure he won't mind if we read his book while we wait."

The children enjoyed Teddy's book so much that they left him one of their chewy chocolate bars.

Before the next bus, three big boys came along.

"Hey," one of them cried. "Here's a bear we can chuck around on the bus!"

The biggest boy made a grab for Teddy.
Whoops! Off came Teddy's arm.

"How was I supposed to know his arm was loose?" complained the biggest boy. And he delved into his pocket for his Wonder Knife.

Carefully and very gently, the biggest boy put Teddy back together. "Better than he was in the first place!" he beamed.

All day long the people who met Teddy wondered if he would be all right. When they got off the bus that evening, they couldn't wait to see if he was still there.

"Oh!" they all said in turn. "He's gone!"

But then they spotted a note:

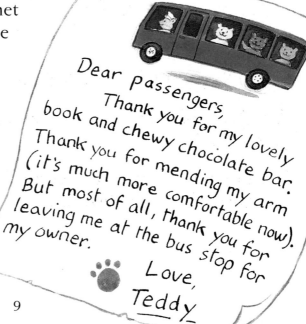

Dear passengers,
    Thank you for my lovely book and chewy chocolate bar.
    Thank you for mending my arm (it's much more comfortable now).
    But most of all, thank you for leaving me at the bus stop for my owner.
                    Love,
                    Teddy

9

Birthday Bear

"That's the end of your story, Sally," said Mum. "Now snuggle down with Bear and go to sleep."

"I'm too excited to sleep," said Sally. "I can't wait until tomorrow."

"I know," said Mum. "There are going to be lots of surprises."

Bear listened with sudden interest. Surprises! He liked surprises, too.

Sally lay awake for a long time, tossing and turning and thinking and wondering. But at last she drifted off to sleep.

Bear, however, was still doing a lot of thinking and wondering of his own.

As soon as everyone was asleep, Bear slipped out of Sally's arms and slid down onto the floor.

"I'll start with the cupboard under the stairs," he said to himself.
"That's a good hiding place for surprises."

It was dark and crowded in the cupboard, so Bear had to rummage
around with his paws.

"Coats and scarves, boots and shoes, cans of old paint, umbrellas…"
he muttered. "But no sign of any surprises."

He rummaged some more.

"Brushes and brooms, a teapot, a beach ball,
an old hat… Oh! And a big parcel wrapped in
pretty paper and tied with a ribbon!"

Bear paused…

"A parcel... Parcels mean presents, and presents mean surprises. So this must be a surprise," he decided.

He looked longingly at the parcel, wondering what was inside. But he didn't open it. "If I open it, it won't be a surprise any longer," he said to himself. So, reluctantly, he turned away from the cupboard.

"Perhaps I'll look in the kitchen next," he decided. "There may be an eating sort of surprise in there."

In the kitchen, Bear tried the cupboards first.

"Pots and pans, bowls and plates, cups and saucers, but no surprises," he said sadly to himself.

He tried the fridge next.

"Butter and milk, yogurt and eggs, tomatoes and lettuce... Oh! And a huge cake covered in pink icing, with sugar teddies dancing round the side!"

Bear thought for a moment. *A special cake... Special cakes with pink icing mean special occasions, and special occasions mean surprises. So this must be a surprise!* he decided.

But Bear was puzzled. *What is the special occasion?* he wondered.

Bear thought and thought. "I give up," he said to himself at last. "I'd better look in the dining room next. There may be a clue in there."

Bear pushed open the door and looked around.

"Table and chairs, knives and forks, plates and glasses. No surprises here."

He looked again.

"Oh! And balloons and funny hats!"

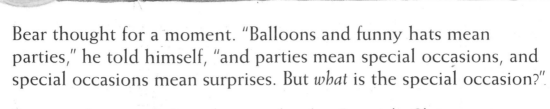

Bear thought for a moment. "Balloons and funny hats mean parties," he told himself, "and parties mean special occasions, and special occasions mean surprises. But *what* is the special occasion?"

Bear sat down and thought even harder. *It can't be Christmas — I haven't seen a Christmas tree...*

He thought some more. *I wonder if it's... could it be...?* Suddenly Bear tingled with excitement.

"Yes! That's it!" he said, jumping up. "It must be... it's got to be... my birthday! And Sally and her mum want it to be a surprise for me!"

Bear smiled a big smile as he climbed the stairs. *I'd better go to bed now*, he thought. *Tomorrow is going to be a big day for me.*

Next afternoon, Bear watched as Sally put on her party dress and party shoes. He was bursting with anticipation.

14

My big moment, thought Bear as Sally carried him downstairs.

The dining room was full of children wearing the funny hats and playing with the balloons. Oh! And there on the table Bear could see the wrapped-up present. Next to it was the cake with the pink icing and the sugar teddies dancing round the side.

That's funny! thought Bear, as he counted the candles on the cake. *I didn't know I was five.*

At that moment, all the children started singing:

> *"Happy birthday to you,*
> *Happy birthday to you."*

Bear listened happily.

> *"Happy birthday, dear Sally,*
> *Happy birthday to you!"*

Bear couldn't believe his ears. It was *Sally's* birthday, not his. This was the wrong sort of surprise! It was awful.

All the children were laughing and shouting. Sally was smiling. Bear felt disappointed, sad and forgotten.

Then all at once Sally announced, "I'm going to blow out the candles. And my special friend Bear is going to help me." She tied the pink ribbon from the parcel in a big bow round his neck, and gave him a pink party hat.

Bear brightened up. He hadn't been forgotten after all!

Sally took a big breath. So did Bear. All five candles went out with one puff.

Or was it two?

"Happy birthday, Sally!" cried the children. "Well done, Bear!"

Bear grinned to himself. He felt very smart in his party hat and bow. And he felt proud to be Sally's special friend. It was a happy surprise after all.

17

Teddy and the Talent Show

Teddy and Tom were excited. They were about to watch a talent show.

"I do hope there'll be a trick cyclist," said Tom.

Well, I want to see some real magic, thought Teddy. And he peered out from his tip-up seat.

The first act was a group of singers. They were very good, and Teddy tapped his paw while Tom hummed to the music.

Next came a comedian. Tom couldn't stop laughing at the jokes. And Teddy nearly fell off his seat.

Then Tom got his wish, and a trick cyclist sped onto the stage.

"Wow!" whispered Tom. "I can barely balance on two wheels, let alone one."

And I still need three and a knee, thought Teddy.

The next act was a troupe of dancers. Teddy and Tom looked at each other and yawned. But there was still one act to follow.

"Now, last," boomed the voice of the presenter, "but by no means least," he added cheerfully, "I give you… *Malcolm the Magician!*"

Teddy sat bolt upright. And when Malcolm asked for a volunteer from the audience, somehow Teddy's arm shot up with all the rest.

Malcolm pretended to take a long time choosing. "The young man in the striped dungarees," he announced at last.

First Teddy was put in a special box.

"Ooooooh," went the audience. It looked just as if Malcolm was sawing Teddy in two!

Then he made him disappear...

and reappear with a rabbit.

In fact, Teddy helped Malcolm with all his tricks. At the end of the act the applause was deafening.

That night Mum asked Tom if he had enjoyed the show.

"Oh, Mum," cried Tom, "it was... *magic!*"

And Teddy couldn't help but agree.

The Teddy Bear
Who Couldn't Do Anything

The teddy bear rested his head on the pillow and looked at the toy shelf. The other toys didn't say hello, or smile, or even nod. They never paid any attention to him. They thought he was just a silly old bear who didn't know how to do anything.

Perhaps they're right, thought the teddy bear, looking at the other toys. *The soldier knows how to march. The ballerina knows how to dance. The monkey can play the drum. But all I can do is lie here.*

Up on the shelf, the soldier was getting ready to march. He straightened his shoulders and stood tall as he stepped forward.

The teddy bear watched the shiny soldier march proudly across the shelf. He swung his arms and tapped his heels and turned smartly each time he came to the edge.

"Perhaps I can stand straight and tall and march like the soldier," said the teddy bear, sitting up. "In fact, I'm *sure* I can."

The toy soldier stopped marching and stared at the bear. "What did you say?" he asked.

"Well," said the teddy bear quietly, because suddenly he wasn't so sure of himself, "I could try."

The teddy bear rolled off the bed and tried to march. But his legs were too fat and his tummy was too big. He took three small steps and fell down.

The other toys laughed as the bear climbed back onto the bed.

Then the ballerina began to dance. Round and round she twirled.

The teddy bear tried to dance like the ballerina, but he was much too clumsy. He fell down with a thud, and felt very foolish indeed.

There must be something I can do, the teddy bear thought as he pulled himself back onto the bed. But as hard as he tried, he couldn't think of a single thing.

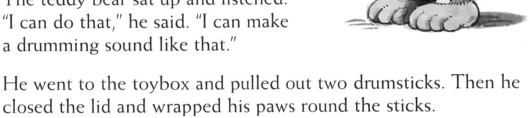

Just then the monkey stepped forward and started to play his drum. *Tap, tap,* went the drum. *Tap, tap, tap, tap, tap, tap.*

The teddy bear sat up and listened. "I can do that," he said. "I can make a drumming sound like that."

He went to the toybox and pulled out two drumsticks. Then he closed the lid and wrapped his paws round the sticks.

Tap, tap, went the drumsticks on the toybox lid. The teddy bear smiled. At last he had found something he could do.

25

But then the sticks slid out of his fat little paws and fell to the floor.

The teddy bear shook his head and sat down in the corner.
"It's no use," he sighed. "I really can't do anything special."

He sat in the corner for a long time, while the other toys marched and played and danced. Then he climbed back into bed and slid down under the covers.

When the sun set and the room grew dark, the little soldier led the ballerina and the monkey back to their places on the shelf. Soon it would be time for the boy to come into the room.

At last the boy turned on the light.
He walked over to the toy shelf.

The soldier stood tall and proud.

The monkey held his drumsticks tightly.

The ballerina was on her toes, ready to dance.

But the boy shook his head. He walked over to the bed and looked on his pillow. Then he looked under the bed. The boy's face grew worried and sad.

Finally the boy got into bed. But he couldn't sleep. Something was wrong.

And then the boy's toe felt something—something soft and round and fat and nice. He reached down, deep under the covers, and found... his teddy bear.

The boy hugged the bear and was happy.

And the bear who couldn't do anything but hug was happy, too.

Midnight in the Park

You know the bear from Number Nine,
She likes to play at night.
Down the drainpipe watch her whizz,
There's not a soul in sight.

She tries a cartwheel on the grass,
She longs to stretch her paws.
Then on the swing she starts to sing,
"It's great to be outdoors!"

"Psst!" Someone's creeping up the path,
They want to try the slide.
It's Twenty-three and Seven B:
"We couldn't stay inside!"

Now Twenty-two is coming too,
And Seventeen and Four,
They're jumping off the climbing frame,
Then running back for more.

But suddenly a light appears,
"What's going on out there?"
A small boy cries and tries to see,
"And where's my teddy bear?"

Up the drainpipe, home they go,
Before it starts to rain,
They leave the park all still and dark,
But they'll be back again!

The Teddy
Who Wanted a T-shirt

Sandy looked in the mirror in disgust.

"Same old velvet waistcoat. Boring old spotty tie," he grumbled. "I must be the worst-dressed bear in town."

Later that day, Sandy's owner had a visitor. And Tess had brought *her* teddy.

When they were introduced, Sandy wriggled in his wretched waistcoat. He squirmed in his terrible tie. Because the visiting teddy looked terrific… in a trendy new T-shirt.

That evening Sandy stuffed his tie down the side of the chair. He turned his waistcoat back to front.

"But it still doesn't look like a T-shirt," he growled.

The next day, Sandy's owner went shopping. He came home with a carrier bag full of new T-shirts.

Mum suddenly got brisk and busy. "We'll pass on all your outgrown T-shirts," she announced. "But first we must give them a wash."

Sandy's owner parked him on the washing machine and ran out to play.

Sandy looked on with longing as Mum loaded in the T-shirts. "Ooooh, look at those lovely stripes!" he sighed.

No sooner had Mum disappeared than Sandy shuffled to the front of the machine. Gingerly, he leaned over the edge to look for the STOP button.

If only I could rescue just one T-shirt, he thought to himself. But everything looked so strange upside down. And, instead of the STOP button, Sandy's nose nudged the EXTRA HOT button.

Later, when Mum unloaded the machine, she squealed in surprise. Because every single T-shirt had been shrunk… to *exactly* Sandy's size!

A Stitch in Time

"Cheer up, Teddy!" began Rabbit.

"It's a lovely, sunny day," went on Dog.

"And you should be happy!" finished Cat.

"But I *am* happy," Teddy told them. "It's just that my mouth turns down at the corners. And I can't do anything about it."

"Good heavens!" cried Cat. *She* had a smile as wide as her face.

"Do you mean you were *made* that way?" grinned Dog and Rabbit together.

Teddy nodded sadly. "However happy I feel inside," he explained, "I always *look* miserable. If only I had just a small smile, then I'm sure Boy would spend more time with me."

That night, when Teddy was asleep, Rabbit, Dog and Cat lay awake. At last they came up with a plan.

Next day they told Teddy what he must do.

"Will it hurt?" he asked.

34

Rabbit, Dog and Cat shook their heads. "Not much," they said.

After supper Boy had his bath.

"Just look at this T-shirt!" cried his mum. "It's almost torn in half."

And with that, she opened the bathroom door and threw the T-shirt across the hallway. It landed in the mending pile.

"*Now!*" cried Rabbit, Dog and Cat.

Teddy leaned over the edge of the bed. "*Ouch!*" He bounced onto the floor, across the hallway and straight on top of the mending pile.

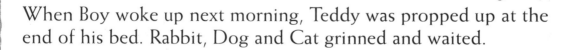

When Boy woke up next morning, Teddy was propped up at the end of his bed. Rabbit, Dog and Cat grinned and waited.

"And what are *you* smiling about?" Boy asked Teddy.

Teddy didn't say a word. He just smiled back.

"Come on," cried Boy suddenly. He grabbed Teddy and leapt out of bed.

"It's a lovely, sunny day. And we're going to play outside together... *all morning!*"

What a Teddy Bear Needs

In a toy shop, on a shelf, sat a row of brand-new teddy bears. They all had fluffy brown fur. They all had big button noses. They all had bright red ribbons round their necks. And they were all smiling.

Except for Eddy Teddy. Eddy Teddy never smiled.

"You need to smile," the other bears told him. "If you don't smile, no one will ever want to take you home."

"I don't need to smile," Eddy said proudly. "I have the fluffiest fur and the biggest nose and the brightest ribbon. I'm the finest teddy bear in this shop."

Just then, a little boy and his mother came into the shop. All the teddy bears sat up straight and smiled their biggest smiles. All except Eddy Teddy. He just sat there.

"I want that one," the little boy told his mother. He pointed to the bear just to the left of Eddy.

What a silly boy, thought Eddy. *I've got fluffier fur than that bear!*

Then a little girl and her father came into the shop. "Please, may I have that bear?" she asked her father. She pointed to the bear just to the right of Eddy.

What a foolish girl, thought Eddy. *That bear's nose is much smaller than mine!*

More and more boys and girls came into the shop. One by one, they each picked a teddy bear. But no one picked Eddy Teddy. Soon he was all alone on the shelf.

I'm not going to sit here and wait any longer, Eddy decided. *I'll go out and find someone to take me home!*

He hopped down from the shelf and left the shop.

Across the road, there was a big park where boys and girls were playing. Eddy saw one little boy playing with a very old teddy bear.

"Hello," said Eddy, walking right up to the boy. "My name is Eddy Teddy, and I will be your new bear."

"No, thank you," said the little boy. "I already have a teddy bear."

"But I'm a much better teddy bear!" Eddy said. "I have the fluffiest fur and the biggest nose and the brightest ribbon. I'm the finest teddy bear in the world!"

"But my teddy bear has something you don't have," said the boy. And he walked away, hugging his old teddy bear.

Then Eddy saw another little boy playing with a tatty old teddy bear.

"Hello," said Eddy. "Wouldn't you like a nice new teddy bear?"

"No, thank you," the boy said. "I'm happy with my own teddy bear."

"But your teddy bear doesn't have fluffy fur, or a big button nose, or a red ribbon," Eddy told him.

"I don't care," the boy said. "He's got something better."

39

Then Eddy saw a little girl playing all alone. She was the prettiest girl Eddy had ever seen. She had yellow hair and big blue eyes. He hurried over to her.

"Hello," said Eddy. "Do you want a teddy bear?"

"Yes, I do," said the little girl.

"Well, here I am!" said Eddy.

"No, thank you," the little girl said. "You're not the right teddy bear for me."

"Why not?" asked Eddy. "I have the fluffiest fur and the biggest nose and the brightest ribbon!"

"But you don't have what a teddy bear really needs," the little girl said sadly.

Eddy was puzzled. He was sure he had everything a teddy bear needed.

Then Eddy saw a rose bush. *That must be what I need*, he thought. *A big red rose for my bright red ribbon.* So he jumped into the rose bush to get the biggest rose.

"Ouch! Ouch! Help!" The thorns pricked Eddy all over. He was stuck inside the bush and he couldn't get out.

The little girl with the yellow hair grabbed Eddy's ears and pulled him free.

"Oh, dear," she said. "You've lost your button nose."

That wasn't all. Stuck to the thorns were bits and pieces of Eddy's fur. And waving from a branch was his bright red ribbon.

"Oh, no!" Eddy cried. He turned away from the little girl and ran all the way back to the toy shop.

On the shelf sat a row of brand-new teddy bears. When they saw Eddy, they shook their heads. "You look terrible!" they said.

Eddy wanted to cry. Now no one would ever want to take him home.

Just then the shop door opened. In walked the yellow-haired little girl with her mother.

All the teddy bears sat up straight and smiled. Except for Eddy Teddy. He hung his head in shame.

"Hello," said the little girl.

Eddy looked up. The little girl was standing right in front of him. She smiled.

And Eddy couldn't help himself. He smiled right back.

"That's the teddy bear I want," the little girl said.

Her mother was surprised. "But he doesn't have fluffy fur or a red ribbon or a button nose," she said. "Why do you want him?"

"Because he has the nicest smile," the little girl said, taking Eddy down from the shelf.

Then Eddy knew what a teddy bear really needs. A teddy bear doesn't need the fluffiest fur or the biggest nose or the brightest ribbon. All a teddy bear needs is a great big smile.

And as the little girl hugged him tightly, Eddy Teddy knew that he would go on smiling for ever.

Seven Sporty Bears

Monday's bear runs far and wide,
Tuesday's bear can bike and ride.

Wednesday's bear plays ball with me,
Thursday's bear can climb a tree.

Friday's bear *will* jump in puddles,
Saturday's bear is best at cuddles.

But Sunday's bear, I'm proud to say,
Has just scored a goal…
Hip, hip, HOORAY!